HAVEN

A SMALL CAT'S
BIG ADVENTURE

HAVEN

A SMALL CAT'S BIG ADVENTURE

Megan Wagner Lloyd

CANDLEWICK PRESS

Text copyright © 2022 by Megan Wagner Lloyd
Title page and epilogue illustration copyright © by Suzie Mason

First edition 2022

Library of Congress Catalog Card Number 2021948367
ISBN 978-1-5362-1657-8

22 23 24 25 26 27 LBM 10 9 8 7 6 5 4 3 2 1

Printed in Melrose Park, IL, USA

This book was typeset in Granjon.

Candlewick Press
99 Dover Street
Somerville, Massachusetts 02144

www.candlewick.com

A JUNIOR LIBRARY GUILD SELECTION

For Izzy

1

Haven woke to the smell of rising dough. She stretched into the smell. She uncurled her tail into it. It was a warm and comforting reminder that she was home.

It was this scent, of dough blossoming into bread, that had brought her to Ma Millie in the first place, back when she was a tiny fluff ball of a kitten.

The furthest back Haven could remember was just before that. She was in a dark, cold forest. She could remember the towering shapes of the trees. She could remember their icy breath. It cut through her like a bitter, biting wind and filled her with fear and lonesomeness. She could not remember what the trees had said to her, or even if they had spoken at all. She could not remember how she'd ended up there.

In that tangled forest that reeked of hidden dangers and clawed at her with spindly arms, the scent had tickled Haven's nose like a kiss. It was as if the sun had decided to rise early. Haven had followed that new and hopeful smell.

Away from the haunting trees, she'd stumbled. Thorns pricked her soft paws. At last she reached a clearing with a fence and a garden and a small house. Its windows were bright with golden light.

Haven had slipped through the fence, stumbled to the doorstep, and pulled herself onto the stoop. There she drank in the strong toasty smell of what she later learned was baking bread. There she listened to the thin reedy sound of someone singing. Haven's paws were bleeding and she was too tired to move. She was, however, able to make a single small sound.

"Mew."

It was no more than a glancing whisper of a sound, but Ma Millie had opened the door almost instantly. It was as if she'd been expecting the kitten's arrival all along.

"Well, hello!" Ma Millie had said.

That had been that. It was Haven's rescue from loneliness, fear, and the cold, unfriendly forest. It was the beginning of life with Ma Millie. It was the beginning of perfect happiness for Haven as a strictly indoor cat.

Now Haven stretched one last time for good measure. Then she climbed up onto the kitchen counter.

"Haven!" Ma Millie gripped the scruff of Haven's neck and hauled her out of the mixing bowl. "There's cats, and then there's bread dough, and never the two need meet!"

Haven squirmed out of Ma Millie's grip and padded away. She shook her head, trying to shake loose the flour that clung to her nose and whiskers. She hadn't meant to slip into the bread bowl. She'd only been trying to get as close to that familiar yeasty smell as she could. And to Ma Millie.

Settling on top of her favorite heating vent, Haven licked the flour from her soft gray fur. Ma Millie sang as she worked the dough. Haven loved Ma Millie's voice, even when it skipped and cracked. In fact, that's what made Ma Millie sound the most like herself.

Ma Millie heaved the dough into a new bowl and covered it with a cloth.

"There, there," Ma Millie said, coming over to squat by Haven. "I'm not angry. You know that, my sweet." She gave Haven an affectionate pat. Haven let the title rest on her like a crown: *My Sweet.*

Ahh. Haven sighed happily. Hers was a splendid life. Ma Millie's house was wholly and completely home.

2

The next afternoon, Ma Millie patted Haven as they sat together in the comfy chair. Haven was eating out of her blue bowl, which was balanced carefully on Ma Millie's lap. Ma Millie was stroking Haven's fur down along her spine in just the right way. The late-summer sun smiled warmly through the window.

Each of Ma Millie's strokes seemed to say, *You're safe. I'll take care of you forever.*

They were interrupted by a knock on the door.

Haven dropped to the floor when Ma Millie stood. "We both know who that must be," she said, smiling and carefully setting Haven's bowl aside.

Haven crept under the couch. Ma Millie opened the door. It was, indeed, their closest neighbor, Jacob Levan.

Even though Jacob Levan was always kind to Ma Millie, Haven didn't like it when he came. His presence reminded Haven that there was a whole big world outside. A tall, broad-shouldered man with a thick black beard, he always wore a flannel shirt, even in summer. In winter, he added a big plaid coat. Today his shirtsleeves were rolled up to his elbows, his only concession to the warm day. He was always bringing them something: firewood in the winter, a bag of groceries from town, or, in this case, a bushel of apples.

"Picked them this morning," he said.

"Thank you, Jacob!"

Haven watched shyly from her hiding place as Ma Millie and Jacob Levan chatted. Today they were talking about Jacob Levan's cows. One of them used to be Ma Millie's, before she grew too old to keep livestock.

Jacob Levan himself always smelled a little boviney. In cold weather, he smelled more like wood smoke.

"I tried the treatment you recommended on

Bessie," Jacob Levan said. "And she's doing much better now. Good as—"

Jacob was interrupted by Ma Millie, who had a fit of coughing. It was a dry, crackly cough.

"Hmm . . ." Jacob Levan looked concerned. "When did that start?"

"Oh, it's nothing." Ma Millie was already busy washing the apples. "Just a tickle in my throat. Probably from the change in season. So much pollen!"

Not one to linger, Jacob Levan was soon leaving, cradling the loaf of bread Ma Millie had pressed on him. Ma Millie opened the door to let him out, and Haven shrank farther into the shadows.

Jacob Levan paused and turned. "I almost forgot." With his free hand, he fished something out of his pocket. He held out a small bag with a picture of a cat on it. "Picked this up in town for the kitty."

"Oh, how nice!" Ma Millie smiled. "Haven!" she called. "Come out, Haven!"

Haven crept reluctantly out into the light. The air from the open door was laced with so many scents that her nose wouldn't stop twitching.

"There you are!" Ma Millie held out the bag, and Haven recognized her favorite cat treats. "Look what Jacob got you!"

To Haven's relief, Jacob Levan didn't seem to expect any meows of thanks from her.

"Bye, now," he said. "You call me if you need anything, okay?"

"And use that old phone?" Ma Millie laughed. "You know me. I get along just fine."

Jacob Levan frowned. "But if that cough keeps up, you might want to get in touch with your doctor."

"Oh, I will," Ma Millie said. "Don't you worry."

Ma Millie picked up Haven and offered her one of the cat treats. Haven didn't mind standing in the doorway as much when she was safe in Ma Millie's arms and had something delicious to eat. Together they watched Jacob Levan's big blue truck head down their driveway and turn onto the road. Where, exactly, Haven wondered, did he live?

"Now, aren't we lucky," Ma Millie mused, "having such a wonderful neighbor?"

3

The last golden days of summer slipped into the bright glory of autumn.

The tree just outside Ma Millie's bedroom window had changed from green to brilliant red. Wild goldenrod bloomed rich yellow. Delicate asters showed their violet petals. Normally Haven enjoyed watching these changes with Ma Millie, but Ma Millie's cough had been growing worse and more frequent.

It had been a mild cough at first, popping up only occasionally. Other than having the cough, she had looked well. One day, when Haven was cozily seated on Ma Millie's lap, eating lunch from her favorite blue bowl, Ma Millie's little cough erupted into a spell of hacking and shaking.

Haven's blue bowl wobbled, slipped, and fell to the floor.

SMASH!

With it tumbled Haven. Sure-footed as always, she landed on her paws—but also on a piece of the broken bowl.

Ow!

Ma Millie lurched out of the chair, still coughing. Hands shaking, she poured herself a glass of water. She drank the whole thing down in one go, washing away her cough. For now.

Haven winced as Ma Millie cleaned and bandaged her paw. It throbbed, reminding her of her flight through the forest as a kitten and the thorns that had pricked her then. Once her paw was safely swaddled, she limped away to rest.

Haven curled up but kept her eyes on Ma Millie.

Ma Millie swept and vacuumed until every speck of the blue bowl was gone.

As the days wore on and the trees began dropping some of their bright leaves, Ma Millie's cough came harder and more frequently. Even tall glasses of water or big cups of tea did not seem to soothe it. Eventually Ma Millie was having great chest-shaking fits. It seemed to Haven that each time Ma Millie coughed, more red leaves twirled by the window. It was as if they were being shaken from their limbs by her stormy illness.

Days went by without the scent of rising dough. As the nights grew cooler, there were no cozy fires to curl up by. How long had it been since Ma Millie had gone to town and come back with big bags of food? *Too long*, thought Haven.

Soon every day was a bad day. When the coughs shook Ma Millie, Haven no longer jumped or ran away. She would climb up onto Ma Millie's bundled shape on the couch and tuck herself close.

There she could hear the beating of Ma Millie's heart. There Haven tried to say with purrs and quiet mews the things she couldn't make Ma Millie understand in words: *You'll get better soon* and *It will be okay.*

The things Haven tried to say to Ma Millie during the day felt as frail as dandelion fluff in the cold dark of night. Ma Millie often quieted, her coughs subsiding into fitful sleep. Haven, however, often found herself wide awake, watching and listening. The cold wind whisked down the chimney. The silver glow of the moon sliced through the windows. The trees moaned and groaned, their branches reaching.

Haven couldn't help wondering what would happen to her if she didn't have this safe and cozy home anymore. If she didn't have Ma Millie.

Haven would shut her eyes tight. She would imagine Ma Millie singing. She would picture her own blue dish, unbroken and overflowing with food in the sweet morning sunshine. She would recall the warmth of Ma Millie's lap as she sat, rocking and knitting. She would think of Ma Millie, being well again. How wonderful that would be!

Sometimes this trickery worked, and she fell into a sound slumber. Other times she lay awake until dawn. On those nights, the forest surrounding their small home was a mouth, just waiting to bite.

4

The fox ate another mouse.

She wasn't even that hungry. Food had been plentiful in the forest that summer. Her tracking and hunting skills were so strong that the fall had been bountiful as well. Still, the colder days would be here soon. Then would come winter. Desperate or not, at the moment, the fox felt a duty to eat while she could. After all, she never knew how lean the winter would be.

Or how much prey that accursed bobcat would steal for himself. She'd been smelling the creature in the area lately. She wished he would move along. She had no liking for bobcats. They were one of the few animals of the forest whom she felt were a threat. The fox ate prey because she had to, to survive. Most bobcats, the fox had noticed, seemed to relish it. They didn't just eat to live. They enjoyed hunting and hurting smaller animals.

Come winter, if she needed to, she could always find scraps in the closest human's trash bin, though the tall, bearded human did not throw away much. Still, it was always fun to tease the cows he kept.

She could go to the human town and forage for food there, too. The fox brightened at the thought of it. She loved foraging for dumpster doughnuts and other discarded delicacies. Humans were unpredictable, which kept things lively. There would be the journey to get there as well, which was a nice way of varying the scenery.

The fox swallowed down the last of the mouse.

No, the fox wasn't particularly hungry—not yet, anyway.

But she was bored. Yes, the fox was ever so hungry for an adventure.

5

The bobcat watched the rabbit.

Hop . . . hop . . . hop!

He watched it wriggle its little pink nose. The rabbit was as fluffy as a summer cloud, with a downy round tail like a dandelion puff. Its brown fur camouflaged well on the fall forest floor now, but it would stick out against the snow when winter came. Not that it would live that long, of course.

The bobcat could have killed the rabbit already. Easily. He was having a good time slowly sneaking up on it, step by careful step, instead. He liked watching it hop along and nibble at sticks and bark, as if the forest were a safe place for rabbits. As if the world were a place where a bunny could hope to survive.

The bobcat pounced.

Yes, the bobcat always got his prey in the end. Always.

6

The day came when the wind roared.

Ma Millie seemed worse than ever. Her skin felt hot to the touch, yet she couldn't seem to stop shaking. Haven climbed up onto the back of the couch and pressed her nose against the window. It was as if the wind were trying to strip the trees bare. Haven was glad that the oak leaves still held tight, as if nothing could make them let go.

Ma Millie sighed. Her sigh turned into a cough. "Reckon it's time to call the doctor," she croaked.

Ma Millie reached for the yellowed plastic phone.

Haven couldn't remember the last time Ma Millie had used it. She watched Ma Millie press a series of buttons and lift it to her ear.

"Hello?" Ma Millie's voice shook. "Hello?"

Slowly Ma Millie set the phone back down.

"Wind must've messed with the phone lines," Ma Millie said. "It's possible I should have got a computer or a cell phone or some such nonsense about this place after all." She coughed again.

Haven leaped up next to Ma Millie on the couch and nuzzled right up by her ear. Haven licked Ma Millie's hand.

Ma Millie burned and shivered. "Oh, Haven. I'm in trouble."

There are few who dare to live out here in the forest, without the comfort of the town around them, Ma Millie had once told her. *Hereabouts there's only you and I and Jacob.*

Jacob Levan! Haven perked up. If she could find Jacob Levan, he would follow her home and help Ma

Millie. Maybe even call the doctor. That would solve everything! All this sickness and trouble would be in the past again, where it belonged.

Step number one: she needed to get out of the house. She needed to do it in the light of what was left of the afternoon. Darkness came more quickly these days, and the cloud cover would make it come even earlier.

"Meow." *Wake up!*

"Meow." *Open the door!*

Finally Ma Millie spoke.

"Haven, my sweet."

Good. Now that she finally had Ma Millie's attention, Haven jumped down from the couch and trotted over to the door. *Out!* she meowed. *I must get out!*

Ma Millie watched Haven. "What is it?" she asked. "Do you need something? What do you need, Haven?"

Haven yowled. *Out!*

Then Ma Millie got swept up in another wave

of coughing. When the coughing faded away, Ma Millie fell asleep.

Haven yowled some more. She went over to lick Ma Millie's hand. Ma Millie slept on. Haven glared at the doors she could not open. There was nothing to do but wait.

7

Eventually the wind quieted, but the dark was closing in fast. Haven tried again. She yowled, a long, lonesome plea.

Ma Millie stirred. She looked at Haven through weary eyes.

Haven jumped up onto the sofa and onto Ma Millie and would not stop meowing.

Slowly Ma Millie sat up. She reached up to unfasten the latch of the window behind the couch and opened it.

Cool air rushed in.

"Go on," Ma Millie croaked.

Haven hadn't even considered the window. They'd always gone through the door. But Ma Millie had at last understood that Haven needed to go out, that she needed to go find help.

Now that the window was open, Haven was less sure of her plan. She was only a small cat. The outdoors and the forest were big. She didn't know the way to Jacob Levan's house. Or how long it would take to get there.

Haven took one last look around the room. The fireplace was cold and empty. A plain bowl had replaced her blue one. Before Millie got sick, theirs had been a life of toasty warmth and comforting kindness.

Brrr. Ma Millie shivered. That was all the nudge Haven needed to leave and be done with it.

Before she could change her mind, Haven dropped into the coming night. *Ouch!* One of her paws landed on a poky acorn top. This,

Haven thought, was why she didn't trust the outdoors. Every inch of it was full of dangers big and small.

Above her, the window slid shut.

This was it, then. She was outdoors, in a world that smelled very much like things that would enjoy eating a small cat.

8

The bobcat was tracking a squirrel when he caught a whiff of the fox. *Blech!*

He hated foxes. Sneaky and disgusting, they were—every last one of them. They pretended to be real predators, stealing rabbits that were rightfully his. Then they would turn around and raid human yards and towns. They would stoop to eating birdseed and even dig through trash. The bobcat would never sink that low. He was a forest creature, through and through.

The scent of fox accosted his nose again. It was quite near. It also smelled . . . familiar. This was the same fox, the bobcat realized, who had bothered him before. *This* fox wouldn't leave when he came around. Not like the others. No, this fox stayed put and ate what she wanted. This fox pretended not to be afraid of him. It wasn't right. The fox would surely be even more annoying come winter, when food was harder to find.

The bobcat had left the fox alone so far. He had been distracted by easier prey. Perhaps, he thought, it was time to take care of the fox, once and for all.

The bobcat crept forward. He would kill and eat this squirrel first. Then he would follow the trail of the smelly fox. He was stealthier than the fox. He knew how to move more quietly. He knew how to approach his quarry so his scent didn't carry in their direction. He knew how to stay so low in the underbrush or so high in the trees that even those with the best eyesight wouldn't see him.

The fox would never even know he was tracking her.

9

The world went dark as twilight gave way to night.

At the fence around Ma Millie's yard, Haven paused, her heart hammering.

There was plenty of room for her to slip underneath the lowest of its wooden rails. She had just never done so, not since she had come to live with Ma Millie. She had never wanted to leave.

Jacob Levan, Haven repeated to herself. *Jacob Levan.* She ducked under the fence, leaving the yard.

The trees towered like overgrown shadows. Haven tried not to look at them as she set off down the driveway. The gravel was sharp and uneven under her paws. At the very edge of the road, she stopped again to gather her courage.

The question now was which way to turn.

Ma Millie always turned toward the sunrise when she went to the town. Haven could just barely see her disappear that way as she watched from the window each time.

What about Jacob Levan? Which way did he go when he drove away?

Haven swallowed, trying to remember. She remembered his big blue truck at his last visit. She remembered seeing it turn around in the yard, roll down the driveway, and . . .

She was sure—mostly sure, anyway—that he had turned in the same direction Ma Millie always went.

Haven turned onto the road in the direction of sunrise and began to run.

Roaaaaar! Something was coming! Haven crouched, flattened her ears. Bright lights blinded her.

Whoooosh! The car whizzed by, ruffling Haven's

fur. A pair of red lights disappeared around the bend, and the car was gone.

That was close. She needed to be more careful. Haven moved closer to the grass at the very edge of the road and picked up her pace. Assuming she was headed in the right direction, how would she know when she had reached Jacob Levan's home? What if she ran right past it?

She needn't have worried. The smell of cows and old wood smoke told her she was close. A little farther, and she spotted a break in the trees. She was at the entrance to a gravel driveway. She'd found Jacob Levan's home!

Don't you worry, Ma Millie, she thought. *Help will be coming soon!*

Haven raced up the driveway and slipped under a gate. She ran past a fenced-in pasture and up the front steps of a cabin, square and neat.

"Meow?"

"Meow?"

No one answered.

Then Haven noticed: no smoke sang from the chimney, no lights shone from the windows, no blue truck sat in the driveway.

No one was home.

10

Haven slumped. It simply wasn't right. How could Jacob Levan be gone now, when Haven needed him? When Ma Millie needed him most of all? Where could he be, anyway? It was night, when everyone was supposed to be at home, tucked in and safe from all troublesome things.

The moon at last peered out from shifting clouds, as if to see what Haven would do next. Haven turned away from Jacob Levan's cabin, her thoughts running in circles. Maybe she just needed to look harder. Maybe Jacob Levan and his truck were hidden somewhere else on his property.

A sharp odor led her back to the fenced-in pasture.

The cows! Haven's thoughts brightened. Maybe Jacob Levan was with the cows. If not, maybe the cows knew where he'd gone and when he'd be back.

Haven spotted a cluster of dark shapes at the far end of the pasture and moved toward it.

Ma Millie had once kept one of these cows, back before Haven had first come to her. Ma Millie had gotten, in her own words, "too old and lazy" to keep a cow. So Jacob Levan had come one day and taken it to his property. Haven hoped that the cow would remember Ma Millie and help her.

Cold mud squelched under Haven's paws as she made her way across the pasture. The cows seemed to get bigger—and smellier—the closer she got. There were three of them, all dark red. Haven found them in the middle of a conversation.

"*You're* frightened, but that doesn't mean the rest of us need to be," the largest cow was saying.

"We're *all* frightened!" shrilled the smallest cow. "He should be back by now!"

Haven cleared her throat. "Hello?"

Three huge heads lowered. Three pairs of big glossy eyes, bright in the dark, turned toward her.

"And who is this?" mooed the largest cow.

"A cat?" whispered the middle-sized cow, sounding uncertain.

"No, a kitten!" shrieked the smallest cow. "See how tiny it is!"

A kitten! Haven puffed out her chest and sat up on her hind legs to show just how grown she was.

The largest cow laughed.

"It's *adorable*," trilled the smallest cow.

"It's a cat," whispered the middle-sized cow, sounding more certain this time.

"I'm looking for Jacob Levan," Haven said as confidently as she could. She needed to get to the point. Otherwise she might be here all night, given the way these three liked to talk.

"We don't—" began the small cow.

"He's in town," said the large cow. "He'll be back soon."

"He should have been back by now!" said the middle-sized cow.

"He should have been back yesterday!" said the small cow. "I'm worried!"

"It's like I've been telling you," the large cow scolded, looking away from Haven. "It was probably the windstorm. It probably just held him up a little bit. Or maybe he had trouble with his truck."

The voice of the frightened small cow was still echoing in Haven's ears. *I'm worried!* That was how she felt about Ma Millie. Haven tried to think what to do. She needed Jacob Levan. He was her only hope for help. No other human would understand that she was Ma Millie's cat.

"But Ma Millie is sick!" Haven said, her panic rising. "She needs his help!"

"Ah, Ma Millie," said the largest cow. "She used to be my human! Now she's yours?"

"Yes," Haven said. "And she's sick!"

"What will we do if he doesn't come back?" squealed the smallest cow, still focused on Jacob Levan. "How will we survive?"

"Maybe you could find him for us," the middle-sized cow said to Haven, sounding suddenly hopeful.

"I'm sorry to hear Ma Millie is ill," the largest cow said, ignoring the others. "She's a good one. I think you'd best wait here with us for Jacob."

Haven considered this idea. These cows were trapped inside a fence. They were also slow and lumbering. They didn't seem capable of helping her find Jacob Levan. She didn't think she could just sit and wait. If Jacob Levan was stuck in the town, he could be gone for days. Weeks, even!

Haven had been to the town with Ma Millie once before, when she was a kitten and couldn't keep her food down. The problem was, she couldn't remember how long the journey had taken. Or what the town had even looked like. All she remembered was the pain in her stomach on the way there and the relief she'd felt on the way back.

"Do you know the way to town?" Haven asked the cows. "Or how long it will take to get there?"

The cows stared at her.

"I'm going to do it," Haven announced. "I'm going to find Jacob Levan."

"The road takes Jacob Levan to town, so just keep following the road," the largest cow boomed, "though I don't recommend this journey at all. The frost will be here soon."

Haven bid the cows farewell before she could lose what little nerve she had. As she hurried away, it didn't help that she overheard the middle-sized cow still worrying: "Oh dear, oh dear. She'll never make it to town alive. It's *much* too dangerous, and she's *far* too little to survive."

Even for a full-grown cat, Haven *was* feeling rather small in that moment. Then she heard the small cow's cheery reply: "You just take a good look at that! It's exactly what I'm always telling you: you don't have to be big to be brave!"

It was just what Haven needed to hear to keep going.

11

Haven trotted along the edge of the road, keeping a lookout for cars. Though it was better than the gravel driveways, the surface of the road was still hard and unforgiving. It wasn't long before her paws began to smart with every step. She thought longingly of soft carpet and Ma Millie's warm lap and the safety of a closed door.

Haven eyed the ground next to the road. Thickly carpeted with leaves, it looked softer than the pavement. So she left the road and continued her journey hugging the line of trees. She was uncomfortably close to the forest, but her paws felt much better.

A breeze through the trees made a hissing sound.

Haven's chest tightened and her head buzzed. *The frost will be here soon*, the largest cow had said.

Haven's hunger and tiredness grew. She couldn't remember when she'd last missed a meal like this. She stumbled along, hoping to find a place to curl up and rest, but every spot along the narrow strip of ground seemed too exposed. To one side were the dangers of the road; to the other side were the dangers of the forest.

Haven ventured a little farther and stopped at the sight of something promising, just inside the line of trees: a fallen tree trunk lying across a dip in the ground, forming a small hollow. Such a hiding place might keep her out of view from any prowling thing.

Haven made her way down the embankment, under the fallen tree, and into the hollow, then sank down, hoping she had managed to tuck herself completely out of view.

In spite of her exhaustion, she couldn't sleep. The night was alive with noises.

Creeeeeak.

Scratch!

Whoo! Whoo!

Worst of all were the whispered taunts of the trees. *You don't belong here*, they seemed to hiss. *You come from an easy life. You are no match for the challenges of the outdoors.*

Haven sank deeper into her hiding place, willing the voices to leave her alone.

This forest is wild, called the trees. *You are not!*

12

The fox paced in the dark. It wasn't that she was hungry. She'd just eaten. She wasn't tired, either. The problem, thought the fox, was that everything was too much the same. Sleep, wake. Sleep, wake. Hunt, eat. Hunt, eat. Repeat.

Feeling itchy, the fox sat back on her haunches. She scratched herself with a hind leg. Itch, scratch.

Repeat. If only something interesting or new could happen. She chased a mouse, just for something to do. She tracked a stinky opossum, then left it alone. She dug in the bearded human's trash bin, just because. She would have teased the cows for the fun of it, but they were so busy mooing among themselves that they didn't even hear her provoking growl.

She sniffed the air hopefully. Not the mouse. Not the opossum. Not the trash. Not even the cows. It was something else! *What was that?*

Her nose twitching, the fox followed the trail of *something new.*

13

Haven could barely believe it. She'd survived a night outdoors, alone. Admittedly without getting much sleep. Yet here it was, morning, and she was alive!

Resuming her journey, Haven walked with a little more pride and confidence than she had the day before.

Until, that is, she stepped on a thorn.

Ouch. Haven stopped and sat down. She licked and nibbled and fussed at the thorn, trying to dislodge it from the soft pink pad of her paw. When it finally came out, Haven looked up to find—

A pair of amber eyes staring at her.

Haven jumped back. *Yowl!*

The thing before her came into focus in pieces. *Amber eyes. Pointy ears. Sharp nose. Sharper teeth! And a wild, musky odor.*

Instinct told Haven to run. So she did.

The creature easily caught up with her.

Haven came to a stop and, spitting and hissing, faced the creature. Her ears were back; her heart was racing. She was in a low crouch, all wound up and ready to spring, but certain she was about to die. She tried to scream *Don't eat me!* All that came out was something that sounded like *Eeeee!*

"Interesting," the creature said with a grin, showing sharp teeth. Her voice was raspy, as if—Haven thought—she had the bones of a small animal caught in her throat.

"What a curiosity." The creature sounded pleased, intrigued even.

Haven gave a low throaty growl. It was bad enough that she was about to be eaten. She wouldn't be mocked, too.

"I'm not a curiosity!" she said. "I'm a cat! And," she added before her bravery deserted her, "cats are very fierce!"

"I know you're a cat," the creature said, sounding exasperated. "I've been to town. By the way, the cats I usually chase never just stop like you did. They keep running, spoiled pets. They are scared of foxes."

A fox. Haven had seen such animals through Ma Millie's window. They would slink along the edge of the forest, a splash of bright color against the green. Now here she was, about to get eaten by one.

"You've got more guts than that bunch in town,"

continued the fox. "But you're a pet, too; that much is clear. No wild animal has paws that tender or smells so much like"—the fox sniffed—"flowers."

That would be the shampoo that Ma Millie washed her with on odious bath days, Haven thought.

Haven and the fox stared at each other in a kind of standoff. This gave Haven's mind a chance to catch up with everything the fox had said. *Spoiled pets. That bunch in town*—

Town! This fox had been to *the town*!

Trying not to notice how big the fox was, or the size of her paws, or the glistening brightness of her teeth, Haven rose from her crouch. She stood and met the fox's amber eyes, trying hard to keep her voice from quavering.

"I'm Haven," she said.

"What's a haven? I thought you were a cat." The fox, her expression unreadable, was still staring down at Haven. Those jaws could snap closed around a little cat's neck quite easily.

"I'm both," Haven said. "I'm a cat, and my name is Haven. What's your name?"

Surely it would be more difficult to eat someone you had been introduced to, wouldn't it? "Names are for humans," the fox scoffed. "And cats, apparently. *I* am a fox."

"But you *have* to have a name," Haven protested feebly.

"No," retorted the fox. "I don't."

"Well, what did your parents call you?"

"Curious brat," said the fox.

Haven flinched. She thought of all the nice things Ma Millie had called her. *My darling. My sweet. Haven*, the name Ma Millie had given to her because it meant something.

"I . . ." Haven hesitated. "I could give you a name."

"You can't name me," the fox said with a toss of her head. "I am a wild and nameless fox."

"You said you've been to"—trembling, Haven faltered—"town?"

"Much more than most forest animals. I even got

39

hit by a car once," the fox bragged. "Well, my tail got hit anyway. What I mean is, a little danger doesn't keep me away from town. What would life be without some danger? Boring, that's what."

Boring? This fox certainly had very strange ideas.

"I'm looking for Jacob Levan," Haven continued. "He wasn't home. His cows said he went to town."

"Aha! So you know the sleepy cows!"

"The sleepy cows?"

"That's what I call them. Talk about boring!" The fox barked a laugh. "And they're scared of me, too. As if I could eat anything that big!"

Haven felt small. She didn't want to talk anymore about the fox eating anything.

"If I follow this road," Haven asked, "will it take me to town?"

The fox lowered her sharp black muzzle and eyed Haven. "So, let me get this straight," she said. "You're an indoor cat. You're by yourself. And you're trying to get to a town you don't know and have no idea how to find?"

It did seem ridiculous—impossible even—when Haven heard it all laid out like that. "I'm looking for help for Ma Millie. My human," she added. "She's very sick."

The fox looked at Haven for a long moment. "Well," she finally said, "the road will take you to town, but it's shorter to cut through the forest."

The forest. Haven didn't even like thinking about it. If she went in, how would she ever find her way out? Who knew what awful, creeping creatures lurked in its shadowy gloom?

Haven was about to say, *I'll stick to the road*, when the fox said, "I *might* be persuaded to guide you if you went through the forest."

Haven, surprised, was speechless.

"It would be an adventure." The fox's eyes gleamed. "And I do love an adventure."

Haven wanted to accept the fox's offer. She also

wanted to believe that the creature wouldn't just eat her along the way.

"I imagine you're used to that Ma Milby human—" the fox began.

"Millie," Haven corrected her.

"—presenting your food to you," the fox continued, ignoring the interruption. "Out here in the wild, nothing is given to you. You've got to work hard to survive."

Haven wasn't scared of working hard to save Ma Millie. It was the fox she was scared of. The talk of Ma Millie and food, however, had given her an idea. With a little luck, she thought, it just might work. "If you show me the way to town, then—" She paused, making sure she had the fox's attention.

The fox eyed her. "Then what?"

"Then, as soon I get back home, I'll give you food. From Ma Millie's house. The best food. Cat food *and* human food. I'll bring it outside to the fence and push it through to you."

The fox's eyes gleamed. "Every day?"

Haven had no idea how she was going to sneak food out of the house in the first place, much less every day. Still, if it kept the fox from eating her for the moment . . .

"Every day," she said.

The fox scratched her belly. "All right," she said at last. "I'll do it. I'll lead you all the way to town. Let's go." With that, the fox turned and trotted into the forest.

There was no time for Haven to wonder if she was making the right choice. She hurried after the fox and entered the forest she had always feared.

You're scared, the trees whispered. *You should be. The forest is full of danger.*

14

The bobcat awoke with a yawn. He stretched luxuriously, never minding that he was balanced on a branch: bobcats never slip and fall.

His nose twitched. What was that? He recognized the smell of the fox he was trailing, but another, unfamiliar scent was mingled with it. There was no smell of blood, so whatever creature was with the fox, it hadn't become her prey—not yet, anyway. What forest animal would travel safely, voluntarily with a solitary fox?

The bobcat was curious, mainly for the sake of his own stomach. What could be better than a two-for-one meal?

The bobcat dropped quietly out of the tree, carefully avoiding a muddy puddle—he *hated* getting wet—and put his nose to the ground. No one was better than a bobcat at stalking. And once he started tracking, he never stopped until he had found his quarry. Oh, yes, he'd find these two travelers. He'd outfox this fox. He'd satisfy his curiosity. Then he'd satisfy his stomach. He'd eat them both. Now, that would be a delicious turn of events, indeed.

15

Whoops!

Haven's paw caught on a tree root, making her trip and tumble, head over heels. *Ouch!* The ground seemed to be made of nothing but sharp stones and poky sticks and squirming bugs. *Blech!* She spit out a sour leaf that had somehow ended up in her mouth. She'd worried about the forest being impossibly dangerous, but it was turning out to be incredibly uncomfortable, too! The fox, on the other hand, looked well rested and at ease, though they'd been walking for what felt like ages.

"Come on then," the fox urged. "Got to keep moving!" She peered more closely at Haven. "Unless, of course, you're too tired."

I'm not used to this like you are, Haven wanted to say, but bit her tongue. She couldn't risk being grumpy with her guide.

"I'm fine," Haven said. "Let's keep going." Onward they went, in silence.

By sunset everything in the forest had started to look the same to Haven. This rock, that rock. This tree, that tree. So very many trees.

When Haven stumbled, numb with sleepiness, the fox finally stopped. "Looks like it's time for us to catch some rest," the fox said. "Ma Milby will just have to wait a bit longer."

"Millie," Haven corrected her again.

The fox led Haven to a place where low tree branches crisscrossed to form a sheltered spot. Haven's legs folded, and she fell down in a heap.

Worn out as she was, Haven thought she would easily fall into a deep sleep. Instead, like the night before, she became wider awake as the night grew darker. This time, instead of unknown sounds and unseen dangers, Haven had something much more real and much closer to fear.

The fox lay a few inches away, her back to Haven. Was the fox sleeping? Or was she only pretending to sleep, planning the moment when she would pounce on Haven?

I won't sleep, Haven thought. *I mustn't sleep.* Again and again she told herself, *Don't sleep.* The night unspooled. *Don't sleep.* Her eyes grew heavier. *Don't sleep . . .*

16

Dawn was approaching, and still the cat slept on. It was foolish, the fox thought, for the cat to sleep so soundly next to a hungry fox. Though the fox preferred smaller prey, she would eat something as big as this small cat—even bigger—from time to time. Anyway, she herself would never be so trusting.

But they had a deal.

The fox peered this way and that way, checking for any sign of movement. Her ears cocked this way and that way, listening for the quietest of paws. Her nose twitched, sniffing for the sour smell of bobcat.

She'd first caught the scent of the bobcat late on the previous afternoon. It had been brief and faint, carried by a shifting breeze. The bobcat had been behind them, perhaps not even on their trail. Still, he was closer than the fox liked, especially now, with the cat in her charge.

The fox had to wonder how things would play out if the bobcat *did* track them down. The fox would most likely have to abandon the cat. In an attack, it would be every animal for herself. Letting the bobcat have the cat would buy the fox time, precious time she could use to save herself.

17

It was bright when Haven woke up. Sunlight beamed through the bursts of yellow leaves that still clung to the trees. The morning air, however, was icy cold. At least there was no frost on the ground yet. The day was blue and sunny, so, Haven hoped, it might yet grow warmer.

The fox looked warm enough, curled in a patch of sunshine with her muzzle tucked under her tail and her eyes blinking in the brightness. With her jaw and teeth hidden, she looked content. She even looked harmless . . . *Almost*, thought Haven.

"Come," the fox said, uncurling and stretching "Time to eat." She wasn't meeting Haven's gaze. Instead she kept peering at the forest around them.

Haven's heart began to race. Was the fox thinking about eating her?

"Follow me," the fox said. "We're going to go catch some fish."

Haven perked up. Eating fish meant *she* wouldn't be breakfast.

"Fish for breakfast," Haven said with relief. "That sounds wonderful!" Sometimes Ma Millie gave her fish out of a can. It was delicious.

"Breakfast?" The fox glanced at her. "What's *breakfast*?"

"You know," Haven said. "Breakfast."

The fox shot her a look. "No."

"You know," Haven repeated, disbelieving. "Like breakfast, lunch, and dinner. Mealtimes."

The fox tilted up her nose. "We foxes eat

when we are hungry, without needing to name the occasion."

Haven smelled the wet soil and fresh fish of the stream before they reached it. The damp breeze made her want to run in the other direction. The fishiness—now, that made her want to run as fast as she possibly could toward it.

The stream gurgled and dazzled in the dappled sunlight. It was colder standing right by the water, but Haven fought the urge to back away. She was willing to do almost anything to eat at this point.

The fox eyed the water intently. "The trick," she said, "is to be quick and decisive. If you hesitate, the fish will slip past you."

A moment later, the fox lunged forward. She came up dripping. A fish flopped in her jaws.

Haven moved closer to the water, cringing as her paws sank into mud. She stared at the wavering surface, determined to do her part in catching fish. The stream rushed and babbled by and—

There! Something sleek and shiny!

Haven thrust a paw forward, claws extended. With her paw hovering just above the water, she hesitated. Did she *really* have to get wet?

The fish was gone.

Oops. Haven edged closer to the water and crouched down. Damp, cold rocks pressed against her empty belly. She would catch the next fish. Even if it meant getting soaked to her skin.

A flash of silver—

Haven plunged a paw into the icy water . . . and the fish slipped right past her. She sat back, wet and disappointed.

Splash! The fox dove back into the water and came up with another fish. She tossed it at Haven, then shook herself off, spraying cold droplets.

"It takes a while to learn," said the fox, "so it's faster if I just catch them for you."

"Thank you." Haven felt a little foolish. That didn't stop her from gobbling up every last bite, and even licking the delicate fish bones. She'd never eaten something that had been alive just moments before. Still, it felt wonderful to finally have a full belly.

"We'll reach town in two more sunrises," the fox said.

"Two more days!" Haven couldn't believe her ears. "I thought this was the shortcut!"

The fox was dismissive. "The road would have taken you three."

Haven knew that, even once she reached the town, it would take at least part of another day to locate Jacob Levan. Then there would be the drive back to Ma Millie's in his blue truck. She wished they could get to the town faster. Still, going through the forest had been the right choice.

"Today's biggest challenge," the fox said, "will be the river. Tomorrow's, the ravine." The fox sounded excited, even a little on edge. "Though other dangers may surprise us along the way," she added.

"What about the river will be a challenge?" asked Haven. "And what's a ravine?"

The fox snorted at Haven's questions. "Well,

think of the river as a very wide and deep stream. And a ravine is a steep dip in the land."

Haven wasn't quite sure what to make of those answers.

The fox eyed the treetops. "Let's be on our way. Hurry."

Instead of leading Haven back into the trees, the fox padded down to the edge of the stream. "Here," the fox said. "We'll go down along this way. And then cross the stream. It'll be good practice for you, for the river."

Haven followed the fox, carefully picking her way along the edge of the water and trying to understand these new ideas. She dreaded the *deep river* and the *steep ravine*, and the danger.

The place where the fox made her cross the stream was so shallow that Haven's belly didn't even touch the water. It was still cold on her legs, though, and disgustingly wet. Haven was so busy thinking of Ma Millie, however, that none of it bothered her as much as it might normally.

Three days hammered in Haven's heart as she followed the fox back into the trees. She forgot her wet legs and paws. She forgot about the river and the ravine. She forgot everything but *three days* to get back to Ma Millie.

She barely even noticed how the forest glowed in the sunlight or how quiet the trees were right now. She was so focused on Ma Millie that she barely paid attention when they crisscrossed back over the stream two more times.

Three whole days.

How many coughs would burst out of Ma Millie in three days? How many times would she gasp for air? How much hotter would her forehead grow?

Three three three three three.

18

Ughhh.

Haven had no idea how long they'd been moving. She couldn't recall when running had changed to plodding.

When they paused for a rest, Haven curled and uncurled her tail on the cold ground, trying to get comfortable. No sooner had she sunk into sleep on a pile of damp leaves than the fox, with another glance around them, declared that they must continue on.

The drips of sunlight that spilled through the lacework of tree branches and unfallen leaves faded as the day wore on. They were replaced by sweeping clouds and a gray sky. The towering evergreens shed their prickling needles on the forest floor. A cool wind wound between the tree trunks.

At last they came to the bank of a wide river.

Haven stared at it. It was *much* wider than the stream had been. How could they possibly get across it?

"Follow me," the fox said. "The water may not look fast here, but underneath, the currents pull hard. There's an easier place to cross down here."

Underneath? Haven's ears flattened.

The fox picked her way along the riverbank. Haven followed, trying not to slip. Reeds at the river's edge seemed to reach out and grab at her legs.

"There," the fox said. "The river is shallow in the middle, see?" Haven followed the fox's line of vision to a mound of pebbles glistening under a shallow cover of water. "We can swim to that halfway point," the fox continued, "take a rest, then swim the rest of the way."

"Swim?" Haven repeated.

The fox eyed her. "You can swim, can't you?"

"Um . . . maybe?" Haven wished she could say yes. "I've never tried."

But the fox didn't seem to be listening. She was

looking behind and beyond Haven, as if searching for something. Haven followed the fox's gaze but saw only a tangle of trees.

"Come on." The fox crouched low to the ground. "Climb on my back."

Haven hesitated. While she had grown accustomed to the fox's presence, she still didn't like the idea of being that close to her. It would make her entirely dependent on the fox's goodwill, something that could disappear at any moment.

"Hurry," said the fox, cutting into her thoughts.

Haven reminded herself that she had to do whatever it took to help Ma Millie. Plus, maybe on the fox's back she wouldn't even get wet. She clambered up. "I'll bring you extra food this winter just for this," she said for good measure. "Ma Millie always has loads of good things to eat."

"You'd better," the fox said.

Haven snicked her claws into the tangle of the fox's fur to hold on more firmly.

Splash! They plunged into the cold sweep of the river. Icy water closed over Haven's legs and even her back. They bobbed up and the fox paddled on, her movements careful and swift.

Haven tried not to look down into the murky and unknowable depths of the water. She tried to fix her gaze on the opposite shore instead.

The fox swam with strong, dogged strokes. Even so, they were carried down the river. The shallow strip of pebbles seemed never to grow any closer. Haven wound her paws and claws tighter.

"Almost there," the fox gasped.

Fear sat heavy in Haven's chest. She closed her eyes tight. *The river's too strong. The shore's too far away. I'm weighing us both down—*

The fox's movements suddenly became clumsy. Haven opened her eyes to discover that they were no longer swimming but climbing up onto the tiny island. She could hardly believe it.

The fox dropped to her haunches to catch her

breath. Haven untangled her claws from the fox's fur and slid off her back. Her legs wobbled. Yes, she was standing in cold water and on a bunch of rocks. Yet it seemed like a temporary paradise.

"We'd better get going," the fox said, eyeing the darkening sky. She stood and shook water from her fur.

Every bit of Haven rebelled at the thought of going back into the river, but the fox was waiting, so Haven climbed back on.

Back into the water they went.

"I can *just* about touch the bottom." The fox half walked, half swam through the water. The other side of the riverbank came closer, closer . . . just a little bit farther . . .

Just as the fox was about to climb out of the river, "Whoa!" she cried, slipping.

Haven was thrown off the fox's back and into the fast-running river.

Water was everywhere. It filled Haven's throat

and nose. It blocked up her ears and blinded her with muddy gloom. A paw scraped sandy ground. She'd found the bottom. Before she could get her footing, the current swept her away.

The river tossed her over sunken logs and tumbled her over rocks. She swallowed great gulps of water. She coughed and gasped and caught the sound of barking . . . and then was pulled under again.

What had she been thinking, going on this journey? She wasn't strong enough. She wasn't used to the outdoors. She didn't know how to swim. She didn't know how to fish or catch her own food.

The trick, she remembered the fox saying, *is to be quick and decisive.* The thought dangled before her like a rope that could tow her to shore. *QUICK! DECISIVE!*

Haven kicked and clawed with a burst of stubborn determination. Her head broke the surface.

Kick! Kick! Kick! She was staying afloat. She couldn't tell which way the shore lay, but she wasn't sinking anymore. *I'm swimming!* she realized.

"Over here!" a voice called over the rush of the river.

Haven scanned the water and spied the brown-red of the fox, bobbing toward her.

"Look at me!" Haven cried. "I'm swimming!"

The fox swam up alongside her. "This way!"

Haven obediently followed the fox. *Kick! Kick!* How much farther would she be able to manage? She was cold and tired.

Her front paws hooked solid ground. She stumbled out of the river and onto the shore, just behind the fox.

"Thank you," Haven wheezed, then promptly coughed up a lungful of river water.

How Haven longed to be curled up on a warm heating vent right now or snuggled on Ma Millie's lap.

"We need to keep going," the fox said.

Haven looked at the fox. The creature had helped her swim out of the river today when she could have just let her drown.

"I was wondering," Haven began.

"Hmm?" The fox sounded distracted. "What?"

"Do you have a home?"

The fox flashed her a look. "What's a home?"

"You know," Haven said. "A home. Like, a place that's just your own. Or your family's. Where you're safe."

"Life's not safe," the fox said. "And all of the forest is my home."

Haven sighed. Maybe their lives were too different for her and the fox to ever be able to relate to each other.

It didn't matter. All she had to do was make it through this night and another, and then she would be at the town. Then she would find Jacob Levan. Together they would drive home to Ma Millie.

So onward she went, though her legs and lungs protested. By the time they stopped, Haven could barely put one foot in front of the other.

"You go inside first." The fox nodded at a hollow log.

Haven climbed in obediently. She curled up at the end, where the log was blocked by debris. The fox climbed in after her, staying close to the entrance and looking out.

Haven found the log cozier and much warmer than sleeping on bare ground, and less exposed. That night, she didn't even mind the sound of the wind in the trees' branches—not like before. The trees were growing more familiar to her, almost harmless.

Hold on, Ma Millie, Haven thought. *Hold on.*

19

The fox didn't sleep. She was on alert, listening for the slightest cracking of a twig, catching every scent, watching for a pair of yellow eyes.

The fox figured she could get herself out of any scrape, or most of them, anyway. And even when the forest did claim her, as it would eventually . . . well, then that would be that. It was different, feeling responsible for someone else's life.

Glancing at Haven, the fox tried to push away her worries. Asleep, the cat looked even smaller and more vulnerable than ever.

The fox ground her teeth, suddenly annoyed. What was the pet thinking, going on this journey? She wasn't meant for risks such as these. Why, she'd practically drowned today!

Well, they would just have to be that much more careful.

As the night wore on without a hint of the bobcat,

the fox found herself letting her guard down, just a little. Surely the combination of the stream and the river would have knocked the wild cat off their trail.

We're safe, the fox thought, *for now*. Though she knew that it was impossible for an animal to ever be truly safe in the forest.

20

"Get up." The fox prodded Haven. "We've got to get through the ravine today."

Haven opened her bleary eyes and followed the fox out of the hollow log. The fox had spoken brusquely and didn't seem overly friendly this morning. Still, Haven had to ask, "What's a ravine again?"

The fox didn't answer at first. She didn't even seem to hear the question. She was busily looking all around them, as if searching for something. Haven repeated herself.

"Think of it this way." The fox's ears twitched. "First we'll go very steeply downhill—and then we'll go very sharply uphill again."

Haven didn't want to admit that she couldn't quite picture it.

The sky showed blue, but between emptier branches than the day before; the trees had lost more leaves. Haven hated to think how quickly the day was coming when every last leaf would have fallen.

Fortunately Haven didn't have time to dwell on the future, not with the quick pace the fox kept them at all morning and into the afternoon.

"Here it is," the fox finally said. "The ravine." She was standing on a small rise with only sky behind her. The trees had abruptly thinned. Haven stepped up to stand beside the fox and found herself on a rocky overlook.

The ravine, Haven thought, looked like the deep cuts Ma Millie made in her bread loaves, but on a giant scale. Rocks, trees, and plants fought for space and a hold on the steep downhill slope before them. On the other side of the ravine, the same struggle appeared to be waged on a sharp uphill rise.

They were going to have to pick their way down . . . then all the way back up again. Haven didn't want to think about what would happen if one of them slipped. Haven scooted back from the edge.

The fox, however, began scrambling down through loose clusters of white and gray rocks and rubble. "Come on!" she called back.

Haven began her slow descent. Every step sent pebbles and dirt sliding down with her. One wrong move could send her tumbling, bouncing from rock to rock, breaking one bone after another.

Back home, Haven had liked jumping from the kitchen countertop to the floor. She'd landed just right, many times. Now she eyed a big rock below her. It wasn't really that far away. A shorter distance than the drop from countertop to floor, actually. Maybe some things she had learned indoors could be useful outdoors.

Focusing on the rock, she leaped—

And landed lightly!

Pleased, Haven eyed a tree growing from straight out of the ravine wall and jumped again. This time she landed at the base of the trunk. Bracing herself against it, she looked for her next landing spot.

"Watch this!" she called to the fox, who had fallen behind her now.

Leap!

Haven slipped a little on loose stones but still stuck her landing. She glanced back, expecting the fox to be impressed.

"Don't get too far ahead!" the fox called instead, a note of warning in her voice.

I'm ahead, thought Haven. It was satisfying, the idea that she might be better than the fox at something out here in the wild.

Leap!

Haven's spirits lifted as she descended. The air was crisp, and the jagged shapes of the rocks were clear against the blue of the sky.

Leap!

Haven soared from rock to tree to rock, pausing occasionally for the fox to catch up. She didn't want to end up at the bottom all alone . . . but was careful to maintain her enjoyable lead.

At last, Haven took one last leap and landed at the bottom of the ravine. She looked up at the walls rising and curving up on either side of her. She felt like she was being held by a huge pair of rocky hands.

The fox picked her way down to the bottom. "Well done," she said to Haven.

Haven beamed. She had a feeling that the fox did not give compliments easily.

"Best not to linger," the fox added. "Better to be back up in the shelter of the trees on the other side as soon as possible. And watch out for hawks," she added, turning to begin the climb up the other side.

"Hawks?" Haven squeaked. "Why didn't you tell me before?" Her pride at getting to the bottom first melted away. To think that she could have been stolen away by a hawk when she'd rushed ahead!

"I didn't think of it before," the fox said. "I'm too big to interest them, for the most part. Unless they're really hungry. You're small enough that one might try to carry you away. If you see or hear one coming at you, dive under a rock and I'll try to scare it off."

Haven eyed the sky, wary.

"Stay close," the fox said. "We'll look larger together."

The way up and out of the ravine was much more difficult than the way down had been. Going downhill Haven had been able to use the slope to her advantage. Now she fought against it at every step. She was careful to stay right next to the fox, keeping a watchful eye trained on the sky. Every sound made her start, convinced a hawk was about to snatch her away.

Step by step, she managed to keep up with the fox. Together they made it all the way to the top of the ravine. With a growl, the fox pulled herself up over the edge. With a pant, Haven followed. She felt readier for a nap than ever before.

The fox glanced at her. "No sleeping yet. First, we eat . . . And then we go a ways farther."

Haven sighed.

"There's a berry patch right around here," the fox said. "It's the tail end of the season, but with no frost yet, there just might be a few mouthfuls still. Come on! It'll be"—the fox hesitated—"breakfast!"

Haven blinked, surprised. She couldn't help enjoying the fox's unexpected use of the human word. She didn't point out that it must be more like dinnertime by now.

They hadn't gone far when the fox stopped in front of some brambly bushes and sniffed deeply several times. Then she said, "Come on!" and disappeared into a small gap in the tangle.

Haven squeezed through the same poky, narrow opening. When she came out on the other side—scratched and bleeding in several places—she found herself in a small clearing. It was ringed by thorny bushes that boasted a sprinkle of red berries.

Haven stared. *Raspberries!*

Ma Millie sometimes brought home the pinky-red berries, and Haven would get to taste them right out of the warm scoop of her palm. She couldn't eat too many of them—they were tricky on her belly—but what she could eat, she adored.

The fox was already eating. Haven searched for a berry. There was only a smattering left this late in the year.

There was one! It plopped easily off and into her mouth. *Yum!*

Mixed with the flowery smell of the berries, Haven smelled another odor. It was unfamiliar, musky, and overpowering. *A hawk?* she worried.

Haven looked around for the source and found it. A huge, shaggy, hulking creature was looming over her.

GRRRRR!

It was definitely not a hawk.

21

Fear dropped over Haven like a net.

The huge creature growled again, a deep rumble that made Haven tremble.

The animal was massive. It was bigger than Ma Millie, bigger than Jacob Levan even. It had thick, dark fur; small beady eyes; and teeth that made the fox's fangs look positively harmless.

"Out," the creature said. "These are my berries."

Relief made Haven swoon. If all the creature wanted was the raspberries, she would be more than happy to leave. If only she could make her legs move.

"Hey there, bear!" The fox was suddenly between Haven and the creature.

"Oh, it's you," the bear said, sounding annoyed. "Fox."

"We're sorry," Haven said. "Of course these are your berries."

The bear glared at the fox. "See? Your oversize squirrel friend sees that it's *my* berry patch. Go on, then. Get out of here."

The fox glared back. "The forest belongs to no one, *including* these berries."

"These are the very last berries of the season!" the bear roared. "There aren't enough for all of us! Do you have any idea how hard it is to eat enough food to keep myself alive while I sleep *all winter*?"

The bear shoved its muzzle right up into the fox's face. "And if I don't get to eat every last one of these berries, I might be hungry enough to eat anything that gets in my way! Now, get out!" The bear rose up on its hind legs, opened its gigantic jaws, and—

RAWWWWRRRRR!

Haven needed no other encouragement. She turned and darted back through the brambles. She could hear the fox right behind her. They burst out on the other side and kept on running.

Haven felt like she'd lived nine whole lives by the time they stopped. The sun was sinking toward the treetops, and the temperature was dropping.

The fox twitched her ears. "You know what?"

"What?" Haven said, panting.

"I think you might be onto something with your whole naming thing. I name that bear"—the fox looked mischievous—"Greedy Grumpsalot."

Haven twitched her whiskers. "Greedy Grumpsa-lot!" she repeated. "It's perfect."

As Haven and the fox walked on, an orange sunset bloomed around them. Haven thought maybe there was something to be said for the fresh air and sunshine and endless spaces of the outdoors, after all. It wasn't that she liked it, exactly. It was just . . . interesting, somehow. It made her feel very alive.

Night came, a full moon beaming down like a friendly face.

"We're almost to a good sleeping spot," the fox said.

A sound grew—a lapping, swishing sound. Like the stream, but louder. Haven hurried onward, despite her tiredness. She was curious.

"There," the fox finally said. "What do you think of that?"

Haven walked up to stand beside the fox and stopped, stunned. "Wow," she breathed.

Before them a pool of water reflected silver moonlight. Above it, a waterfall tumbled down, sending ripple after ripple through the pool. Huge rocks, mossy and shiny, supported the waterfall and held the water in the pool like a giant bowl.

Haven walked toward the water. At the edge of the pool, where the water was relatively still, she stopped and peered down. She couldn't see through to the bottom. A scattering of leaves, metallic in the moonlight, floated on the surface. And there—

That's not me, Haven thought. *It can't be!*

Haven stared at her reflection. Gone was the sweet fluffy cat who had feasted on food from a blue bowl. *This* cat looked like a creature from the underbelly of the forest. Her paws and legs were matted and mud-caked. Her fur was tangled and torn. Why, even her beautiful tail was ragged! Nothing about her was sleek or well-kept.

Would Ma Millie even recognize her? Would Jacob Levan?

The fox's reflection joined Haven's. "Let's get some sleep."

Trying to shake off her troubled thoughts, Haven followed the fox into a small cave in the rocks near the waterfall.

"Haven?"

"Mm-hmm?"

"I'll wake you up before daybreak. Then we'll head into the town."

"Okay," Haven said. "'Night."

"'Night." Before long, the fox's breathing slowed.

The waterfall tumbled, the ceiling of the cave dripped, the night grew colder, and Haven realized that—for the first time—the fox had called her by her name.

22

The fox, certain that they'd left the bobcat behind, slept soundly at last. Still, she wasn't one to sleep for long. She was awake again in the darkness and patrolling the area around the waterfall while Haven kept sleeping.

It had been getting a tiny bit colder each day. Tonight was the coldest yet. Luckily they were close to the town. Close enough that the fox could almost taste delicious dumpster doughnuts. Soon, she thought with satisfaction, she would have completed what some might have thought impossible: safely shepherding a nearly helpless animal to town. Though she had to admit, Haven had surprised her at times. She'd shown bravery and determination.

Not that any of that would have helped if that bobcat had found them.

The fox thanked her lucky stars that they'd managed to escape the bobcat so far. Maybe the bobcat had been tracking other prey all along. Maybe their paths had intersected only by chance.

The fox nosed along the ground, searching for . . . *breakfast*, she thought. Then felt silly for thinking it.

Sniff . . . sniff . . . Was that a mouse?

The fox froze. Her fur stood on end. She *had* smelled a mouse. She had smelled a stronger scent, too. The bobcat. Still close by.

23

"Hurry." The fox's voice was urgent. "We need to move. Now."

Still sleepy, Haven tripped out of the cave, her breath appearing before her in white puffs. The sky was a dark blue that would soon shift into dawn. The edge of the waterfall's pool, she noticed, was lacy with ice. The first frost had finally come.

Fall is fading, Haven thought, feeling suddenly sad. The raspberries they'd found just yesterday would be frozen . . . unless the bear had gobbled up the rest of them.

Somewhere nearby, an owl hooted a sad, sweet lullaby. Frost had traced paths on the fallen leaves, turning the forest floor silver. When, Haven wondered, had the world become so beautiful?

They rounded a boulder and stopped short as six deer, who had been tearing at tree bark, swiveled their heads. One of the deer had a big spread of antlers. Twelve shining eyes fixed on them as they quietly passed by.

As dawn turned the sky pink, Haven and the fox reached the end of the forest.

Haven could hardly believe that they were almost there. That she was so very close to finding help for Ma Millie.

Before them, a field of long, brittle grasses sloped away toward a cluster of houses and roads and buildings. The town looked like the humans' very own lumpy, bumpy forest. It was bigger than Haven had expected. How strange it was to see so many houses all bunched together. Finding Jacob Levan would be an even bigger task than she'd been able to imagine.

"Best to get there before many humans are out and about," the fox said. She seemed pleased about leaving the forest behind, but Haven found herself glancing back. The thin sprinkling of red and brown leaves left on the trees caught the morning light and seemed to be winking goodbye.

She and the fox would be parting ways soon. The fox's side of the bargain would be fulfilled.

The fox.

"Hold on." Haven stopped. Glancing curiously at her, the fox slowed to a stop, too.

"Do you think—" Haven began. She started over. "Is there a name I could start calling you? I mean . . . only if you want."

"Hmm . . ." The fox paused. "I say if Greedy Grumpsalot gets a name, then I should get one, too. But it'd better be a good one."

Haven agreed. The fox should get a meaningful name, a name that captured their time together. The fox had helped Haven. The fox had stuck to their bargain. The fox had been true to her word.

True. Now that was a good word. Would it be a good name?

She looked at the fox. "How about True?"

"True," repeated the fox. "I like it."

Haven straightened her tail and lifted her head high. "I name you True."

True grinned.

24

Grrr. The bobcat growled in frustration.

Just when he'd finally found the trail of the fox and her companion, they'd left the forest completely and gone into town! He hated to admit it, but the fox was no fool.

Well, he was no fool, either. He wasn't about to go mixing himself up with humans, but he would stick around, keep his eyes peeled. He knew the fox wouldn't stay with the humans for long. Foxes needed the forest as much as he did.

The fox, he knew, would come back.

When she did?

The bobcat purred.

He'd be waiting.

25

Now that they'd actually entered the town, Haven felt overwhelmed by all the houses and roads. The pavement was rough under her paws as she followed True across a parking lot.

It was surprising to Haven how easy it was to think of the fox by her new name.

True disappeared into a big stinky garbage container she'd called a dumpster. Haven waited, all sorts of salty and sweet smells calling to her.

True's head reappeared, a pink box gripped by her jaws. She dropped it out of the dumpster. *Whump!* The box landed next to Haven.

"Breakfast!" True announced, leaping down to

join Haven. She tore at one corner of the box, ripping it open with her teeth.

"Oh!" Haven recognized the treat. "Doughnuts!"

Six doughnuts filled the box like eggs in a nest. Haven took a small nibble. True snapped up half a doughnut in one bite. Haven watched True eat, her stomach churning. Was it the sugary doughnut making her feel bad? True polished off three doughnuts, then gave a contented sigh.

Was this goodbye? They did have their deal about Haven bringing food to the fence once she was back home with Ma Millie, but that felt so far away. She hadn't even found Jacob Levan yet.

Haven wanted True to say something. She wanted this to feel like a real goodbye. True's attention, however, had returned to the doughnuts.

"I guess this is it then," Haven said, feeling pitiful.

"I guess it is." The fox didn't look up. "So long!"

Haven took a few steps away, but she just couldn't

leave it at that. Even if the fox didn't care about having a proper farewell, *she* did.

"True?"

True looked up, pink frosting on her muzzle. "Yes?"

"Thanks for showing me the way to town."

True's teeth flashed. "It's been a good little adventure. Not a bad way to pass a few days. Not bad at all. It's been . . . fun, actually."

"I'll see you later at Ma Millie's," Haven said. "Bye!"

"Bye," True said.

Haven walked away, her eyes on the ground. She wondered why she still felt unsettled. It wasn't as if True were going to say, *I want us to stick together.* That wouldn't be like her. Besides, Haven knew it wasn't safe for True to be walking around the town in broad daylight. The fox had told her that humans wouldn't react well to that at all. A cat, on the other hand, was more familiar.

"Haven!" True called, her voice muffled.

Haven looked back at the fox, who had a frosted doughnut hanging from her mouth.

"Good luck!"

"Thanks!" Haven called back. Before she could lose her nerve, she walked away. It was time to find Jacob Levan.

26

Haven looked for Jacob Levan's familiar black beard and plaid coat as she moved through the town, which had begun to stir. There were all kinds of humans: big and small, short and tall, far more than Haven had ever expected. How was she going to find Jacob Levan among them all? As the bigness of the town pressed down on her, Haven felt smaller and smaller.

She watched cars and trucks go by, hoping

to see Jacob Levan's blue truck among them. She watched and watched, but didn't see a single blue truck.

What if I do? Will I be able to stop it? she wondered. How would she get the attention of Jacob Levan without being hit by a car? She hoped she would see him in person instead, on a sidewalk.

Haven paced past homes with small patches of fading grass and between buildings twice as big as the houses.

She squeezed under fences. She watched humans go in and out of houses. Children in coats and hats played and raced. A human sitting on a bench threw bread crumbs for birds. She searched every face she passed. When she got close enough, something was always all wrong.

The sun rose higher. The day wore on. Haven ran down what seemed like every street in the whole town. Her paws ached from hard sidewalk.

Haven searched until night fell, the streets

emptied, and the windows of the houses glowed golden. There was no sign of Jacob Levan.

It's useless, Haven thought. *I'll have to wait to try again tomorrow.*

Scriiiitch!

Haven's fur stood on end. *What was that?*

It was only a piece of trash scuttling past, blown by the wind.

Haven crept under a set of rickety wooden steps leading to a darkened house. Lonesomeness squeezed at her heart. This wasn't the way it was supposed to work out. She was supposed to find Jacob Levan today. She was supposed to be back with Ma Millie by now.

If only True were still with her. Together, they probably would have already found Jacob Levan.

27

True tore another bite off the discarded chicken carcass. *Ahh!* Town life was the easy life. Humans threw away so much that was perfectly delicious to eat.

True still preferred the forest, however. She loved its fresh air and endless trails, its leafy trees and scattered sunshine. Which was why she was already on her way back to it. She'd brought the chicken carcass to the edge of the field that led to the forest. She would head back in as soon as she'd eaten. After the morning doughnuts—and saying goodbye to Haven—she'd stayed hidden for the day, only coming out for more scavenging once darkness had cloaked the town.

True picked the bones clean. She should be moving on. She should stop thinking about that little cat.

A light on a nearby metal pole flickered and buzzed. True didn't think she would ever get used to the way the humans tried to light up the night, as if they were trying to turn it into day. In the forest, nighttime was like looking down into a rabbit burrow, the world turning as velvety dark as packed earth. Except when there was a bright moon, of course, like during her travels with Haven last night—

True shook her head. There she was, thinking about her journey with the little cat again! Most adventures, True knew, had only one hero. She, of course, had been the hero on the journey with Haven. She'd led the cat through a river and a ravine. She'd saved her from a bear and, most impressively, from the unseen bobcat. She'd brought Haven safely all the way to town.

True sighed. Her time helping Haven was over. She needed to move on. She should go back to the forest, and quickly.

And yet . . . True scratched her belly with a back leg, as if she could scratch away her circling thoughts.

Maybe this whole naming business was part of the problem. She had agreed to be named to humor the cat, but now caught *herself* thinking of herself as True!

And maybe leaving Haven alone in town to fend for herself had left the adventure unfinished. Would the cat be able to survive the town without help? Humans could be skittish about any hint of the wild in their tame towns. Haven didn't exactly look like a pampered pet anymore. Not only that, but the frost had returned last night, it had stayed cold all this day, and a bitter wind seemed to promise an even chillier night tonight.

True set off, her nose to the ground. But instead of heading back into the forest, she would retrace her steps, sniff out Haven, and make sure she'd survived her first day in town. With any luck, the cat would be gone, already scooped up by the human she'd been looking for, already home, already returned to her life as a pet.

At this point, True would do anything to shake the worry that wouldn't leave her alone.

28

Haven wiggled her nose. *Mmmm . . .*

A smell—golden and warm and familiar!

I'm home! The thought was like a bright bubble of happiness. Her eyes flew open—

Not home. Only the splintered underside of a staircase. Haven remembered: she was still in the town, still searching for Jacob Levan, the only human who knew that Ma Millie was the very best human of all.

Haven sniffed again and smelled baking bread. That part hadn't been a dream. She crawled out from under the stairs into the faint light of the new morning. She was so stiff with cold that it was difficult to move. At least the stairs had protected her from the worst of the night's wind.

Haven followed the aroma down the street. Lights were on inside a few of the buildings. Haven stopped in front of the one with the smell. She climbed up onto the windowsill and peered inside. Behind a counter, two humans in white aprons were hard at work.

Push, slap! Push, slap! One human was kneading a big ball of dough. The other was sliding a risen loaf into an oversize oven. More dough was in bowls or shaped on trays, rising. The human who'd slid a loaf into one oven pulled a tray of crisp and golden loaves out of another.

Haven gazed at the warm scene, her breath clouding the glass. She felt hungry for home, starving for the sound of Ma Millie's singing as she kneaded dough. She even missed Ma Millie's gentle reprimand when Haven made a mess of things.

Renewed determination filled Haven. She had to find Jacob Levan.

First, though, she had to eat something, to give her the strength to keep going.

Haven set out to look for a dumpster, like the one True had dragged the doughnuts from. She let her nose lead her to a trash bin as big as a bear. Mostly it reeked of rot, but something fresh and savory was laced in with all the foul smells. Haven climbed a pile of cardboard boxes stacked haphazardly next to the bin. From the top box, she leaped for the bin's lid. The boxes, jarred by her jump, toppled over. Something metallic clanged in the morning quiet.

Above, a window slid open. "Hey!" a voice shouted. "Go away!"

Haven wanted to run from this grumpy human, but she was ever so hungry. *I'll be quick*, she thought. She struggled with the lid, trying to maneuver it further open. It was difficult to open something she was also sitting on. *Come on . . .*

"I said go away!" yelled the human. "Filthy stray!" Something whistled down from above, and before Haven could react—

WHACK! A boot collided with the bin. The bin wobbled.

"Yowl!" Haven screeched, sliding off the slick plastic. Falling—

OUCH! She landed all wrong on one of her legs.

Haven limped away, trying to decide where to go next. *There!* A parked car just a little ways on. No flying objects could hit her if she was beneath a car.

The car's shiny paint reflected a blurred, twisted version of herself. Quickly Haven crept under the car and crouched on the cold asphalt.

For so long, back in her life before Ma Millie had gotten sick, Haven had been afraid of the forest. Yet now that she had journeyed through it and now that she had experienced the town, with its rumbling cars and trucks and smelly garbage and clomping humans, she longed for the trees. She saw now that they had always been living, breathing guardians, holding her and Ma Millie and their small house close, trying to keep them safe.

29

"Haven?"

A shadowed form appeared in the gap between car and street. Two pointed ears, a long muzzle, sharp teeth—

"True?" Haven's voice cracked.

True squeezed under the car. "Hello."

Haven stared. "How'd you find me?"

"Just followed my nose," True said. "I'm not good at tracking for nothing. Now, come on, let's get you out of here."

"I can't." Haven's voice sounded small, even to herself. "I hurt my leg."

"What happened?"

"I fell."

"Can you walk at all?"

"Maybe a little," Haven said.

"If you can walk at all, let's go. We have to find a better place than this for you to rest up. Hiding out under a car in the day rarely comes to a good end."

True scooted out onto the pavement, and Haven joined her, trying to keep her weight off her hurt leg. It felt good to turn her troubles over to True for a little while. She didn't have to decide what to do next. She just had to follow.

True led her around to the back of a tumbledown shed. They were at the very edge of town now. Only a field lay between them and the forest.

Haven rested her leg, gazing at the forest: trees as far as she could see. She recalled the way sunlight filtered through the layered branches, the way leaves danced in the autumn breeze. She could almost hear the burble of the stream. She could almost smell the deep richness of the dark soil and the bright spice of the evergreens. Haven breathed in the clean, crisp air that seemed to be coming straight from the trees themselves.

The one thing she could definitely hear was the

tap, tap, tap of her own half-tame, half-wild little heart. She'd been through so much. She and True were still alive, yes, but everything else had gone all wrong. Ma Millie was still sick and alone. She had not been able to find Jacob Levan. Had this whole journey been for nothing? Had it been a mistake all along?

Even if it had been, could she give up now? No. She couldn't. She wouldn't. She would go back to Jacob Levan's. He would probably be back home by now. He would know her as Ma Millie's cat. She would lead him to Ma Millie's. He would follow her.

"True," Haven said at last, "I don't think Jacob Levan is in town anymore."

"Do you think he's gone back home to the cows?" True asked.

"Yes, back home," Haven repeated. "I have to get back there."

The fox eyed her. "With that leg?"

"I can walk," Haven said. "I'll be fine."

"I'll come with you," True said.

As they stepped back into the shelter of the forest, Haven welcomed the solid strength of its tree trunks, the crackle of its carpet of leaves, the protection it offered from the wind.

With their progress slowed by Haven's injured leg, it took all morning for them to make it as far back as the waterfall.

The waterfall was half frozen now, with the rest of its fall slowed to drips. The pool below it had iced over almost completely. Only a small circle of inky water still gleamed in the center.

"It's too cold to rest," True said. "I say we keep moving. What do you think?"

Haven was surprised to be asked her opinion. "Keep going," she agreed. Her stomach grumbled loudly. "When we get back to Ma Millie's, I'm going to get you as much food as I can."

True flashed her teeth. "Like doughnuts?"

"If Ma Millie has some," Haven declared. "Doughnuts and bread and cake. Pies and cupcakes and cookies. And fish from a can. And—"

RAHHHHRRRR!

30

Something slammed into True, knocking her flat. For a confused moment, Haven thought the fox had been hit by a falling branch.

But *no*. The thing holding True down was no fallen branch. This thing was alive. It had long whiskers and pointed ears and yellow eyes and wicked teeth and was twice as big as True.

"I've been waiting for you," the bobcat said, grinning down at True. Then it slashed its claws across True's snout.

True yipped in pain and surprise, then snarled and sank her teeth into the bobcat's leg.

The bobcat hissed.

True and the bobcat became a great writhing mass of claws and teeth. Haven's head spun with the smell of blood.

Pounce! The bobcat knocked True to the ground.

The bobcat is trying to kill True, Haven realized with horror.

Howling, Haven threw herself at the bobcat. She sank her teeth into one of its legs, tasting flesh and feeling bone.

The bobcat kicked, trying to shake her off.

Haven sank her claws into the leg, too.

Growling, the bobcat released True, then turned on Haven. The bobcat dug its claws into Haven's back, yanked its leg out from between her jaws, and flung her to the side.

WHACK! Haven hit a tree trunk and slid to the ground, dazed.

Haven tried to see what was happening to True now, but all she could see was the bobcat, coming after *her* again.

Slash! The bobcat raked its claws across her face.

Snap! Haven tried to bite the bobcat again, but it was already heading back to True.

Haven blinked. Something was wrong with one of her eyes. With her working eye, she saw that True was struggling to stand.

Rawr! The bobcat attacked the fox again, a fury of snarls and claws, until True went still upon the ground and did not get back up.

Haven felt smaller and more useless than the tiniest pebble. First she'd failed Ma Millie. Now she'd been too weak to help True. And her eye . . . What was wrong with her eye?

She could see well enough, however, to watch the bobcat turn its yellow gaze back on her. It crept toward her. Closer. Closer . . .

What was that? Something behind the bobcat had moved. Or had it? Maybe it was nothing more than the wind stirring the fox's fur. It was hard to tell, with only one eye working.

There it was again! Haven was sure of it. Not all

hope was lost, not yet. She could still do something to save True.

Haven stared at their predator, a completely wild version of herself. In short, an overgrown *cat*. Haven knew a thing or two about being a cat.

Haven stood. Keeping as much weight as she could off her hurt leg, she took a wobbly step to the side, then another.

Haven had caught the bobcat's curiosity. It laughed. "Trying to escape?"

Haven didn't reply. She just kept walking, limping. Not too much farther to go. Good, the bobcat was taking the bait. It stalked her all the way to the edge of the frozen pool at the bottom of the waterfall. She took a step onto the ice, its surface frosted and dark. The cold of it burned her paws.

The bobcat stopped at the pool's edge, but its eyes followed Haven as she stepped farther and farther out onto the ice.

It thinks it's already killed True, Haven thought.

Haven held the bobcat's gaze. *Come and get me.*

31

The little cat glared at the bobcat with defiance. Such a fierce look on such a tiny face was humorous. As if the creature hadn't noticed that one of her eyes was a bloodied mess and that one of her legs was limp and useless. As if she wasn't scared at all of plunging into the freezing cold water beneath the ice.

A new sensation crept over the bobcat, one that he didn't find funny at all. *Fear*, he realized with shock. No—that couldn't be right. Of course not. He was never scared. Of foxes. Of minuscule, insignificant cats. Of ice, of water—of anything.

Clinging to the thought and baring his teeth, the bobcat took a step onto the slick surface. A shiver ran all the way from his paws to his tail, but he took another step, testing the ice. It held. Another step, and another. He was tired of the little cat, of her games. One last blow and the little cat would be done for.

The ice creaked and cracked under his paws, but didn't break. He walked all the way out to face the cat, lifted a paw, bared his claws, and swung.

32

Haven darted to the side just as the bobcat lunged, paw swinging.

Crack! The ice under the bobcat splintered.

Haven stumbled backward.

The bobcat's eyes went wide as it fell into the icy water. *SPLASH!* The bobcat thrashed madly, droplets spraying everywhere.

Haven scrambled back, trying to keep a grip on the ice.

Raaarrrgh! the bobcat cried . . . before it sank into the cold, dark deep.

The bobcat did not reappear.

Haven scooted way from the fractured edges of the hole and made her way carefully back to shore. As soon as she stepped onto firm ground, she was suddenly too weak to stand, overwhelmed by pain, by cold, by fear, by relief. And too overwhelmed to speak.

She looked over at True, still slumped on the ground, her tail twitching ever so slightly. True would recover from her injuries, Haven told herself. She had to.

Haven might not have been able to bring help to Ma Millie. She might not have been able to find Jacob Levan. But at least she had been able to save True. At least Haven had learned what it took to be brave, what it took to be herself, truly.

33

Ow.

True wished she hadn't opened her eyes. Her snout hurt; her head hurt. Her *everything* hurt.

She squeezed her eyes shut again. What had happened to her? To her and Haven—?

True's eyes flew open, remembering. She rose to her feet and fell—*Ow!*—and scrambled up again. *The bobcat!* The bobcat had attacked, and Haven hadn't run away. Oh, why hadn't she run away? True scanned the forest. There was no sign of the predator.

"Haven?" True called, hoarse, frantic, stumbling toward the water.

There, at the edge of the pool . . .

True limped over to the little lump of gray fur. "Haven?" The small cat didn't respond.

True nudged the cat with her nose. "Haven?"

Still Haven didn't answer. Her eyes didn't open. One eye was covered in blood.

All this time, True had been thinking that she was on a grand adventure, a heroic fox guiding a helpless cat.

Haven hadn't been so helpless after all. Somehow, someway, she had gotten rid of the bobcat. Somehow Haven had saved *her*.

True wheezed as she slid under Haven, managing to lift her until the cat lay limply across her back. Legs trembling, True was able to carry Haven to a road, where her strength gave out. With Haven still resting on her back, she lowered herself to the ground, hoping a human would spot them there. Even if they wouldn't help a wild animal like herself, she hoped they would help Haven.

"My friend," True murmured. "Why'd you have to be a hero?"

34

Haven was warm. Deliciously warm. The kind of warm to be found in a kitchen with an oven ready for baking, and heating vents perfect for napping on, and sun-kissed carpets made for stretching.

She was clean and fresh, too, and lying on something fluffy and cushioned and soft. Best of all, someone was patting her back gently, in just the right way.

It was all too perfect to be real.

She wouldn't open her eyes. She couldn't. Not if it meant that this beautiful dream would end. Still, she couldn't resist stretching—

Owwww!

Stretching hurt. Every bit of her hurt. Not only that, but there was something stiff wrapped around one of her back legs. Something also covered one eye, forcing it to stay shut.

As much as Haven wanted to let herself rest in

the warmth and comfort of the moment, she was curious. She opened her uncovered eye—

Ma Millie gazed back at her.

Haven meowed and meowed and licked Ma Millie's hand. She snuggled up close to her, purring.

"My Haven," Ma Millie whispered. Her voice was as thin and crackly as an autumn leaf. "My sweet."

Ma Millie patted Haven's back, ever so gently. Though her hand trembled, each pat said, *I love you.* Each pat said, *You're home.*

They were not home, Haven realized the next time she awoke. This room and this bed were unfamiliar. As was the woman who came in, helped Ma Millie eat a bowl of soup, adjusted her blankets, gave her medicine, and left again.

There was a window at the other end of the room. Through it, Haven had a glimpse of the brown forest and the blue sky, and that made her happy. *Come back*, the trees seemed to wave. *We miss you.*

"The nurse will be back again tomorrow morning," someone was saying to Ma Millie when Haven woke another time. "The goal is to keep you comfortable, so be sure to speak up if you aren't."

Haven opened her working eye. The speaker was sitting in a rocking chair by the foot of the bed. Slowly he came into focus: a big man with a bushy beard and a kind face.

Jacob Levan! So that's where they were—Jacob Levan's house. He must have found Ma Millie somehow after all.

"Thank you," Ma Millie said. She formed each word slowly, as if it took a mighty effort. "How I got lucky enough to have a neighbor like you, I'll never know."

Jacob Levan smiled. "Well, I'm still wondering how your miracle cat was lucky enough to be found by someone with the presence of mind to take her straight to an animal hospital."

Animal hospital? Haven didn't remember anything about that. She couldn't remember anything after collapsing next to the waterfall's pool. What had happened to True?

Ma Millie patted Haven. "Miracle cat, indeed."

Haven kept listening, hoping that one of them might say something about a fox. Had there been a fox beside her when she was found? Had a fox been taken to the animal hospital, too? Where was True?

Instead of the answers Haven longed to hear, Ma Millie and Jacob Levan talked only of boring things. Did Ma Millie want a glass of water? When would the first snow of the season come? All that listening made Haven sleepy.

"Jacob?" Ma Millie's voice was small. "I have . . . I have a favor to ask."

"Ask away."

"Could you take care of her?" Ma Millie whispered. "After . . . ?"

Jacob Levan's voice was gentle. "Of course."

35

In the bright, calm days that followed, Haven drank in everything she loved about Ma Millie: her wispy hair, her wrinkled face, her kind eyes, her smile. When Haven made Ma Millie laugh with her meows and purrs and licks, Haven was sure that Ma Millie was getting better.

Yet in the chill of the night, when the moon was shrouded by clouds and the trees sighed in sympathy, some part of Haven knew the truth. She felt it in the way Ma Millie never spoke of the future. She saw it in Jacob Levan's deep-brown eyes. She heard it in the tired beating of Ma Millie's heart. She saw it in the growing ashiness of Ma Millie's complexion and the amount of time Ma Millie spent sleeping. One dreary morning, Ma Millie whispered, "Haven." Somehow Haven knew what was happening. It was something too sad to believe and too terrible to be real. Her head hurt and her belly twisted.

The nurse and Jacob Levan were in the room, looking solemn. Between them, the window showed bare branches and gray sky.

Haven crept up to nuzzle under Ma Millie's chin and purr, trying to say everything that needed to be said.

Ma Millie must have understood, because she patted Haven softly, just once—*I love you, too*—then let her hand rest there on Haven's back.

Ma Millie's stilled heart left an enormous silence. This time, there was no journey Haven could take to try to save her.

36

The winter was long and cold. Haven spent much of her time lying underneath the bed where Ma Millie had last slept.

She didn't want to eat crunchy cat food in the new orange bowl. Jacob Levan would sit at her side and watch until she ate at least a few bites.

Eventually Haven began to limp around, exploring Jacob's house. It was small and cozy, like hers and Ma Millie's had been, but different. Instead of a fireplace, it had a woodstove. Instead of a blue couch, it had a green one. Instead of baking bread, Jacob liked to make hearty breakfasts of pancakes and bacon and eggs. He was always happy to share with her, offering little nibbles of golden scrambled eggs. "Millie's cat," he often called her, which made her feel both a little bit sad and a little bit happy.

One day, Jacob took Haven in his blue truck to a veterinarian, who removed the stiff wrappings from her head and leg.

To Haven's delight, her back leg, though weak, worked again. Her eye had changed permanently, though. When it was finally uncovered, the world around it stayed dark. Try as she might, Haven couldn't blink it. The eyelid wouldn't move at all. The bobcat had hurt her eye beyond repair.

Haven had to swivel her head farther to see all her surroundings, and she had to rely even more on her senses of hearing and smell. It was difficult.

Still, trying to save True had been worth it. If only she could find out what had happened to the fox.

Now that her leg worked well again, Haven climbed to the top of the green couch and pressed her nose against the cold window. Snow drifted down like the flour Ma Millie used to pour out to make bread. It hid all the harsh edges and softened all the crooked branches.

Day after day, Haven watched for a flash of coppery red. She saw only white.

It seemed like winter was lasting forever.

Hearts, Haven was realizing, could break and go on beating. Day by day and step by step, broken hearts could slowly heal.

37

Every day, Jacob went outside to take care of the cows. Every day, Haven turned away from the open door. She was not ready to face the wide world again.

Until, one day, a hint of freshness swooped in through the open door. It carried the beckoning smells of rich soil and sprouting plants. Quickly, before Jacob shut the door on his way out, Haven ran to him and rubbed up against his legs.

"You want to come along, do you?" He scooped

her up. "The fresh air will do you good. And the cows will be happy to meet you."

Once through the door, Haven peered out from her perch in Jacob's arms, looking for any flash of reddish orange in the patchy snow. She saw only Jacob's blue truck, a few purple crocuses peeking up out of the snow, and the familiar brown trees of the forest.

Hello! The trees waved to her.

Jacob and Haven entered the small barn by the pasture. Three heads turned in Haven's direction. And three sets of kind eyes fastened on her.

"Well, if it isn't—" the middle-sized cow began slowly.

"It's her! It's really her. It's that kitten!" squealed the smallest cow. "I knew she could do it!"

"That's no kitten," said the largest cow. "That, my dears, is a cat."

Jacob set Haven softly down. She hesitated, feeling shy under the cows' enthusiastic attention.

"Go on, then. Say hello." Jacob winked at her. "They won't bite."

"It's time we all met properly," said the largest cow. "I'm Bessie, as you may remember. I was Millie's cow, before your time."

"I'm Clover," said the middle-sized cow.

"Ooh, ooh, let's tell her what we did!" squeaked the smallest cow. "Oh, and I'm Dot!"

"Back in the fall," began Clover, "after your visit, well, our dear Jacob came back—troubles with his truck, you see, had held him up—and then—"

"Then we wouldn't stop mooing!" broke in Dot.

"We made a right racket," boomed Bessie proudly. "We mooed until Jacob said, 'I don't know what's gotten into you three.' Until he said, 'I think I'll go see if Millie ever saw this with Bessie before.'"

"And the next thing we knew—" began Clover.

"He was carrying her inside the house!" squealed Dot. "His house! He was taking care of your Millie!"

"Oh!" Haven sat down with a thump, understanding bowling her over. "Oh!"

"Didn't we do a good job?" Dot chirped. "Aren't you impressed with us?"

"Yes." The barn swirled around Haven. "Yes. You did a great job." She tried to focus on the cows' eager faces. "Thank you so much."

Haven walked in circles through the house the rest of the day, hardly able to believe what the cows had told her. Her journey to save Ma Millie had actually worked. If she hadn't left home to begin with, if she hadn't sought out Jacob and told the cows about Ma Millie, then they wouldn't have mooed. If they hadn't kept on mooing, Jacob wouldn't have gone to Ma Millie's for advice. If Jacob Levan hadn't gone to Ma Millie's for advice, he wouldn't have found her and brought her back to his house to take care of her.

But Haven *had* gone, the cows *had* mooed, help *had* come, and Jacob Levan *had* found Ma Millie. It all started because Haven had decided to jump out the window, slip under the fence, and run into the forest.

Haven held her tail a little straighter and taller. The heavy weight in her chest grew just a little lighter. Her journey had made a difference after all. *She* had made a difference. Ma Millie's last days had been filled with warmth and comfort and love, and they'd both had time to say goodbye.

38

Haven grew restless. She heard the ice crackling as it melted and the birds singing once again. She spotted more tiny crocuses blooming. She paced the house: wall to wall, corner to corner, window to window, and back again.

A part of Haven wanted to stay inside, avoid the memories the outside would bring, protect herself from any bad news she might find out there. Yet when she smelled the forest waking up, it made something inside her wake up, too. She began going out to the barn with Jacob every day. She was better now, for the most part. Not quite the same—no, she'd never be the same. But she was well enough to want to stretch her legs. And she wanted to know what had happened to True. She *needed* to know what had happened to True.

The cows teased her. "You're as jumpy as a mouse!" Bessie mooed as Haven paced around the barn.

At last, one day, instead of following Jacob into the barn to resume her pacing, she ran to the fence, ducked under it, and ran right into the forest.

The melting snow and spring rain had turned the ground to mud. Haven didn't mind. It felt right to be among the strong and steady towering trees. She was a pet who adored the love and safety of a cozy home, it was true. But now she saw herself as a wild creature of the forest, too. She was capable of clawing her way through winter, and fighting and biting back.

On the forest floor, scattered bunches of daffodils tilted their faces up to the sun's warm smile. The trilling of birds filled the air. The beginnings of buds gave a hint of green to the trees' brown branches. Haven breathed, long and deep.

She was all of this, and more.

She was Haven.

EPILOGUE

Spring transformed the world into splashes of flowers and curtains of green. As the weather warmed, Haven went into the forest almost every day. Each time, she traveled a little farther. She always came back.

One day, as Haven was following the fluttering trail of a yellow butterfly, her nose caught a familiar scent. A smell like the trees, like the outdoors, like . . . a friend.

Haven ran. She scrambled over logs and under branches. She dodged tree trunks and tree roots.

There—

There!

Rushing toward her in a red-orange blur—

"TRUE!"

The fox's fur was a patchwork of scars. One of her ears had been torn to shreds. Yet her amber eyes shone in the same old way. "That's my name!"

"But—" Haven said. "How?" With so many questions, she didn't know where to begin.

"Took them *forever* to let me out of that animal hospital," True said.

"It was you," said Haven. "You brought me to the road. You saved me."

True gave her a long look. "I think you've got that backward, Haven."

Side by side, Haven and True romped through the emerald trees. The forest glowed green and sharp and beautiful.

"Maybe you need a different name now," True

said. "Hmm . . . Like Haven the Fierce or—well, we'll think of something!"

Haven laughed. She felt like she could run and run and never stop, like she could run in her forest forever.

ACKNOWLEDGMENTS

Writing *Haven* was a journey that I was able to complete only because of the generous amount of help and support I received along the way.

Thank you to Ammi-Joan Paquette for believing in this story through years of setbacks and for having faith that I would figure it out in the end.

Many thanks to Mary Lee Donovan for bringing *Haven* into the Candlewick fold and for the expert guidance and editorial vision.

Thank you to Analía Cabello for the insightful feedback, Suzie Mason for the beautiful and evocative cover art, and the entire Candlewick team for the hard work and attention to detail.

Thank you to everyone who read and critiqued the manuscript over the years: Rebecca Lynn Sladek, Jay Lehmann, Doug Marshall, Stacey Donoghue, Jason June, and Lucy and Nelle.

Many thanks to my extended family on both

sides for supporting my books, with special thanks to Anna and Steve and to Sam for their constant positivity and support.

Thank you to my parents, who always understood that a bookworm is never done reading.

And the biggest and brightest thanks of all to Seth, Izzy, Lucy, and Nelle. Thank you for sharing this adventure with me and for believing in me over and over again. You are my forever favorites.

MEGAN WAGNER LLOYD is the author of the middle-grade graphic novel *Allergic* and of the picture books *Finding Wild*, *Fort-Building Time*, *Building Books*, and *Paper Mice*. She lives with her family in the Washington, DC, area.